# My Beautiful Child

## LISA DESIMINI

### illustrated by

## MATT MAHURIN

## THE BLUE SKY PRESS

*An Imprint of Scholastic Inc. • New York*

THE BLUE SKY PRESS

Text copyright © 2004 by Lisa Desimini

Illustrations copyright © 2004 by Matt Mahurin

For information regarding permission, please write to: Permissions

Department, Scholastic Inc., 557 Broadway, New York, New York 10012.

SCHOLASTIC, THE BLUE SKY PRESS, and associated logos are

trademarks and/or registered trademarks of Scholastic Inc.

Library of Congress catalog card number: 2003005566

ISBN 0-439-45893-5

10 9 8 7 6 5 4 3 2        10 11 12 13 14

Printed in Singapore        46

First printing, May 2004

Designed by Matt Mahurin

and Kathleen Westray

*For each other*

*L. D. & M. M.*

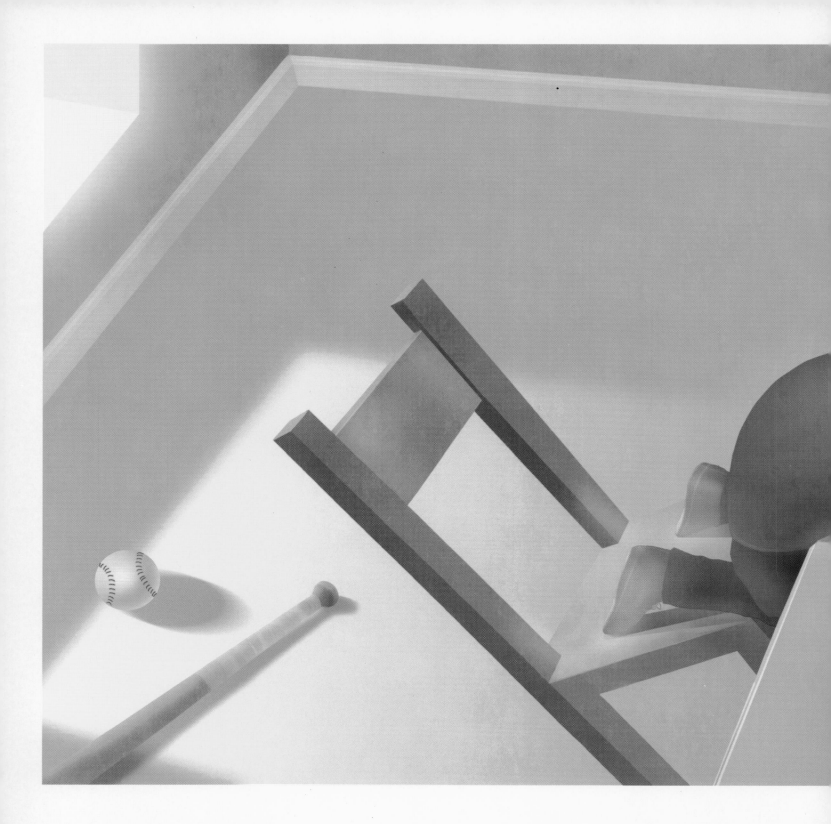

I want to show you everything, my beautiful child.

I want to show you how big the sky is . . .

and how green the grass is.

I want to show you how perfect a flower is . . .

and how soft a blanket can be . . .

how sweet a strawberry is . . .

and how the rain can tickle your face . . .

how warm the sun is . . .

and how a shadow will follow you wherever you go.

I want to show you what was here before you were born . . .

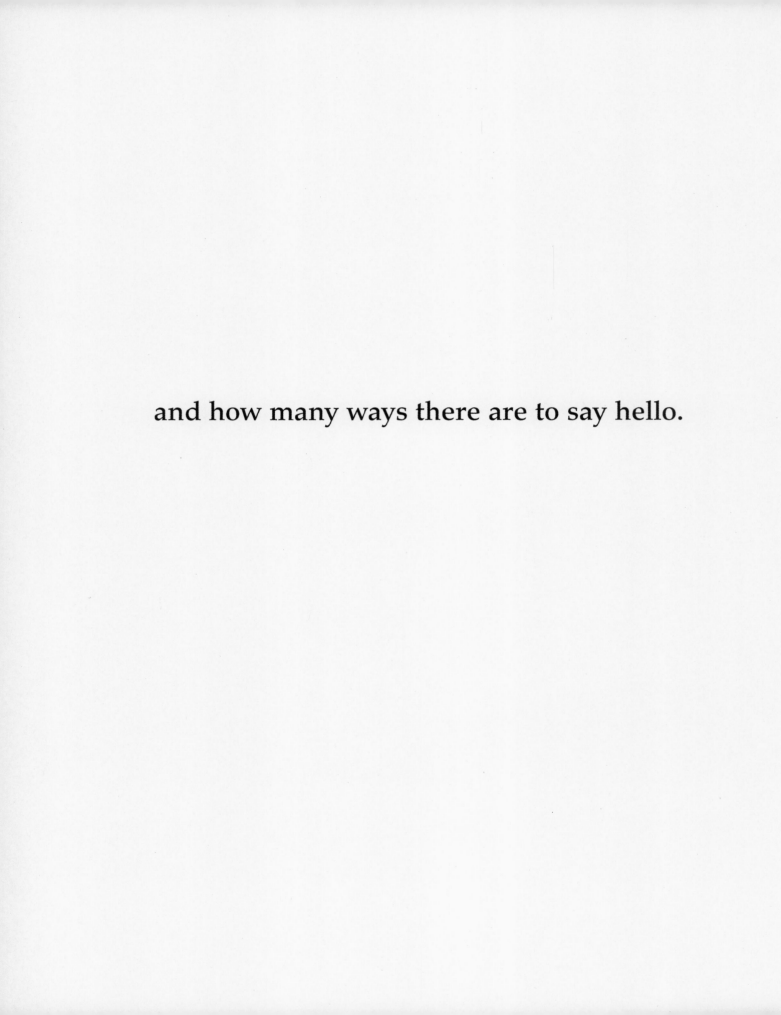

and how many ways there are to say hello.

My beautiful child, how strong your cry is . . .

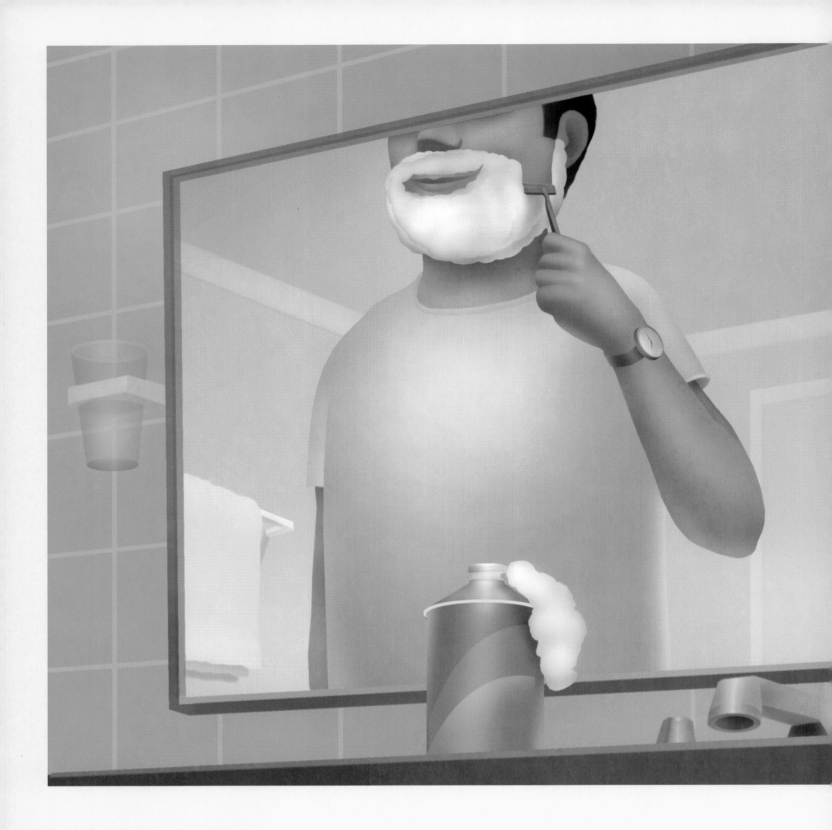

and how bright your smile can be.

I want you to smell a spring day . . .

and crush an autumn leaf in your hand.

What do you see in a dark room?

What do you hear when you're snuggled next to me?

My beautiful child, I want to show you everything . . .

especially how much I love you.